All About
Ella

All about Ella

Ella

Sally Nicholls

With illustrations by
Hannah Coulson

Barrington Stoke

First published in 2022 in Great Britain by
Barrington Stoke Ltd
18 Walker Street, Edinburgh, EH3 7LP

www.barringtonstoke.co.uk

This 4u2read edition based on *All About Ella*
(Barrington Stoke, 2017)

A CIP catalogue record for this book is available
from the British Library upon request

ISBN: 978-1-80090-105-6

Printed by Hussar Books, Poland

To everyone who loved
Ways to Live Forever

CONTENTS

Monday's child is fair of face,

Tuesday's child is full of grace,

Wednesday's child is full of woe,

Thursday's child has far to go,

Friday's child is loving and giving,

Saturday's child works hard for a living,

But the child who is born on the Sabbath Day

Is bonny and blithe and good and gay.

CHAPTER 1
Monday

Fair of Face

It's Monday morning and we're late for school. Mum is in a hurry. Her jumper is on inside out. She hasn't brushed her hair. My big brother is sick and Mum wants to get back home to him.

"Ella, come on now," she says. "We haven't got all day."

She isn't listening to me.

"Mum," I say. "Mum!" I say it again. "What day was I born on?"

We're at the school gate now. The playground is empty. Everyone else has already gone in. Mum stops and looks at me.

"Oh, Ella, I don't know," she says. "What sort of a silly question is that?"

"It's not a silly question," I tell her. "It's a poem. Mr Holly read it to us. Monday's child is fair of face. Tuesday's child is – is ..."

I can't remember what comes next. But when you were born is important. If you know what day it was, then the poem tells you what sort of person you are.

I'm angry with Mum.

"You don't even remember when I was born!" I say.

Mum sighs.

"Of course I remember when you were born," she says. "It was three o'clock in the morning. I was so tired. But I couldn't stop looking at you. You were the most beautiful thing I'd ever seen."

I'm not angry any more. I smile at her.
She hugs me.

"Your jumper's on inside out," I say.

She pulls away and looks at me. Then she sighs again.

"So's yours," she says.

CHAPTER 2
Tuesday

Full of Grace

I have ballet on Tuesday. I don't want to
go. I stamp about the house because I Do
Not Want To Go. Dad tells me to shush or I'll
wake Sam up.

Mum says, "But you love ballet, Ella."

Stamp. That's. Stamp. What. Stamp. You.
Stamp. Think.

Stamp. Stamp. Stamp.

I don't care if I wake my brother up.

He sleeps too much. Even if he is ill.

None of my family cares what I think. Granny comes and takes me to ballet anyway.

"Nobody cares about me," I tell Granny in the car.

"Nonsense!" Granny says as she speeds up to pass a van.

"It is not nonsense!" I say. "Mum can't even remember what day I was born."

"Well, it was a long time ago," Granny says. The van driver is trying to pass us. "Oh no you don't, sonny," Granny says.

"You can't remember either," I say.

"No," Granny says, and she looks at me. "But I know what happened. I was looking after Sam. Your dad rang me up in the middle of the night to say you'd been born. He woke me up, but it didn't matter. He was so happy. He didn't care what time it was."

"He cares now," I say. "If I wake Sam up. I always have to be nice and quiet."

But Granny is passing the van again and she doesn't hear me.

CHAPTER 3
Wednesday

Full of Woe

I bet my brother Sam was born on a Wednesday. He's very ill. And very grumpy.

When I get home on Wednesday, Sam is lying on the sofa with a book. I sit on his feet and turn on the telly.

"Turn that off," he says.

"No," I tell him. "I want to watch the telly." I turn my head away. I do what Mr Holly tells us to do at school. I ignore him and hope he'll go away.

He doesn't.

"I was here first," he says. "And my head hurts."

"It's just TV," I say. "It's my house as much as yours."

I fix my eyes on the screen. Sam pushes himself up and grabs at the remote control.

"No-o-o!" I yell.

Big mistake.

Mum comes into the room and sees me. Her face is red and angry.

"Ella," she says. "Get in the kitchen. Now."

I stamp out of the living room after her.

"It's not fair!" I say before she's even started. "You always let him win!"

Mum shuts the door and turns to me.

"Ella. Listen. Listen to me," she says. "The world isn't all about you. Your brother's very poorly. You know that, don't you? You've got to try and be a good girl just now, while he's ill. Can you do that?"

I don't want to be a good girl.

I don't.

I want to watch telly.

"I hate him!" I shout at her. I shout loud so Sam will hear me. "I wish he was dead!"

Then I run out of the room and up the stairs.

CHAPTER 4
Thursday

Far to Go

On Thursday, no one comes to pick me up from school. My friend Miriam and her mum wait with me at the gate.

"How's your brother?" Miriam's mum says.

"He's fine," I say. "Really good! Just grumpy."

We go back inside and Mr Holly rings home. There's no answer. He rings Mum's mobile. No answer. He rings Granny. No answer there, either. He wants to ring Dad's work, but I don't know the number.

Mr Holly tries all the numbers again and I get more and more scared when still no one answers. Maybe something bad has happened to Sam.

"I expect your mum's stuck in traffic or something," Mr Holly says.

But I think something's happened to Sam.

Maybe it's my fault.

Maybe Mum remembers what I shouted at her yesterday and doesn't want me any more.

Miriam's mum says I can go home with them.

Miriam lives a long way away on the other side of town.

"Did you find out when you were born?" she says.

"No," I say.

"I was born on a Thursday," Miriam says. "At breakfast time."

I look out of the window at the dark streets and I think about Miriam being born at the breakfast table. In between the bowls of cereal. While her dad poured the tea.

It takes us a long time to get to her house.

"It's true what the poem says," I tell her. "You do have a long way to go."

When we get to Miriam's house, we can hear her mum's mobile ringing. It's in her bag, and it's ringing and ringing and ringing. It's Mum. She's at the hospital.

"Are you OK?" she says when Miriam's mum gives me the phone.

"Yes," I say.

"I'm so sorry, sweetheart," she says. "Sam's had to have an emergency blood transfusion. I'm going to stay here with him tonight. Will you be all right there till Dad finishes work?"

"Yes," I say.

Miriam wants to play on the computer, but I don't want to.

I go and watch her mum bake cakes instead. The kitchen smells of cake mix and warmth and chocolate.

Miriam's mum gives me a spoon to lick.

I wonder if you can make people more ill just by wishing.

When at last Dad comes, I run into his arms. He holds me tight.

"It's OK, chickie," he says.

"I thought you were never coming," I say.

CHAPTER 5
Friday

Loving and Giving

I don't want to go to school on Friday, but Dad says I have to. He says he'll finish work early and come and pick me up.

After school, we go to the hospital. As we walk up to the big doors, I get scared.

What if Sam died while I was at school? And it's my fault? What if the police arrest me for fighting with him and wishing he was dead? For saying I hate him, even though I don't really.

I wonder if I'm a Wednesday's child,
who will always be sad and full of woe, or a
Thursday's child, who will be sent far away.

"Dad?" I say. I slide my hand into his.
"What day was I born on?"

"I don't know," he says. "Why?" He sounds surprised. "I can't remember. But I remember driving your mum to the hospital. I drove so fast. I wanted to get here as fast as I could."

"Here? Was I born here?" I say. Now it's my turn to be surprised. I didn't know I'd ever been to hospital. In my family, Sam's the one who goes to hospital, not anyone else.

"Of course you were," Dad says. "Would you like to go see?"

The baby ward is at the top of the hospital. There's a place where we can look in a window at all the babies lying in little cots. They are tiny and soft and red. I wonder what it's like to be so little. I wonder if they're scared, lying there alone without their mums.

"Did I look like that?" I say.

"Just like that," says Dad.

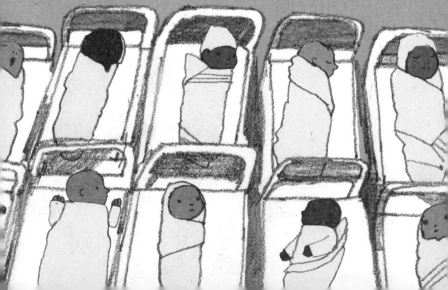

There's a man in the corridor with a tiny baby in his arms. He's smiling and smiling.

"Did you smile when I was born?" I ask Dad.

"Of course I did," Dad says. "Everyone smiled when they saw you. Me and Sam and Granny came to visit you. Granny gave you your ship mobile. Sam gave you Little Teddy."

"Little Teddy?" I'm surprised again. I didn't know he was a present from Sam.

"Everyone had presents for you," Dad says.

I think about this as I stand by Dad.

"Can we buy presents now?" I say.

*

I'm still a little scared, but it's all right. Sam is sitting up in bed talking to Mum.

"Hello," I say.

"Hello," he says.

And Mum gives me a hug and kisses the top of my head.

They like their presents.

We give Mum a mug with a picture of a frog in a top hat and we give Sam a pack of Uno cards.

Dad wanted to buy something boring like bath stuff for Mum. But I said the mug would make her laugh, and it does. She says she'll think about me every time she drinks her tea.

We play Uno on Sam's bed for ages until it's time to go home.

CHAPTER 6
Saturday

Works Hard for a Living

On Saturday, Dad and I get the house ready for Mum and Sam to come home.

We wash up all the dirty mugs and plates. We throw away the fish and chip wrappers and baked bean tins. We hoover the carpet. We buy flowers for Mum and put them in jam jars in all the rooms.

"Sam and I did this before you came home from hospital," Dad says. "Sam was only little.

He wasn't as helpful as you are now. But he was so excited about his baby sister."

It is very cold and the sky is full of clouds as we drive to the hospital.

When we get to Sam's ward, they're packed and waiting for us. Dad carries Mum's bag. I carry Sam's.

The four of us walk back to the car. We're almost there when it begins to snow.

All of a sudden the air is full of snowflakes. We stop and stare. Sam holds out his arms and snowflakes land on them.

I stick out my tongue and lean back as far as I can, trying to catch a snowflake. Snow falls on my face, in my hair, down my back. When a snowflake lands on my tongue, I cheer.

"I got one! I got one!"

Sam laughs. I flick snow at him. He flicks some back at me. There isn't enough yet for proper snowballs, so the snow doesn't go very far. But we don't care.

CHAPTER 7
Sunday

Bonny and Blithe

Sunday is good.

"We should have a party," says Dad.

"A party?" says Mum. "What for?"

"Coming home," says Sam.

"This week being over," Dad says, but he's smiling.

"All right," says Mum. She's smiling too. "What sort of party?"

"Let's have a picnic!" I say. I like picnics.

Mum laughs and looks out of the window.
It's grey and wet outside, and there's
half-melted snow everywhere.

"It's not really picnic weather," she says.
"And no one's been shopping!"

She's right, but me and Sam go to the
kitchen anyway to see what we can find.

We put a rug on the living-room floor and
we spread everything out. We eat golden-syrup

sandwiches and grated-carrot sandwiches
and raisins and cherry-cake cherries and
cornflakes with no milk and crunchy frozen
peas, because everyone knows frozen peas are
nicer than cooked ones.

It's a perfect indoor picnic.

"Ella," Dad says. "Please tell me. Why do
you care what day you were born on?"

"There's a poem," I explain. "Mr Holly read
it to us. It tells you who you are."

"And who are you?" says Dad.

"I don't know," I say. "That's the problem."

"I can find out," says Sam. He is on the
sofa, eating chocolate ice cream from the tub.
He scatters hundreds and thousands on my
head to make me look at him. "It's easy. There
are calendars online. You put your birthday in
and it shows you what day of the week it was."

"Well, there you are!" Dad says. "Shall we look?"

I nod. Dad gives Sam his phone.

All of a sudden, I'm not so sure I want to know. It's all right if I'm a Monday or a

Tuesday child, but what if I'm a Friday and I have to keep giving everyone things all the time? Or a Saturday and I always have to work?

But it's too late to change my mind.

"Sunday!" Sam says. "Bonny and blithe and good and gay. You?!"

Bonny means pretty, that's OK. But good …

"I'm not good!" I say.

"Well," says Mum. "You are sometimes."

"What does blithe mean?" I say. "And gay?"

"Happy," Mum says. She smiles and holds out her hand. "They both mean happy."

She puts her arm around me. I lean against her. I'm not sure about this poem any more. I'm not going to be good just because some poem says I am.

And no one can be happy all the time.

Poems are all very well, I think. And I'm glad I know the answer. But I'd rather just be me.

Our books are tested
for children and young people by
children and young people.

Thanks to everyone who consulted on
a manuscript for their time and effort in
helping us to make our books better
for our readers.

Can you find 6 differences between these two pictures?

Have an indoor picnic

Ask an adult for permission to put a big blanket on the floor and spread out some of your favourite things to eat and drink. Include plenty of fruit and veg. Try to eat a rainbow – here are some ideas.

Red
radishes, tomatoes, strawberries, raspberries, jam

Orange
oranges, carrots, pumpkin, cornflakes

Yellow
peppers, custard, pineapple, sweetcorn, bananas, honey

Green
cucumber, cabbage, broccoli, apples, kiwi, avocado

Blue & Indigo
blueberries, plums, dried cranberries, blue cheese

Violet
purple broccoli, red cabbage, beetroot